MONSTER IN THE CITY

VOLUME 2

JELLABY

MONSTER IN THE CITY

by

KEAN SOO

DISNEP • HYPERION BOOKS
NEW YORK

ACKNOWLEDGMENTS:

SPECIAL THANKS TO CALISTA BRILL, TAMSON WESTON, ROBERTA PRESSEL, AND JUDY HANSEN FOR ONCE AGAIN HELPING TO BRING THIS BOOK TO FRUITION.

AND HUGE THANKS TO *TEAM JELLABY* FOR PROVIDING COLORING ASSISTANCE ON THIS BOOK: NASEEM HRAB, STEPHANIE YUE, ALISA HARRIS, ALISON WILGUS, DIK POSE, JIM ZUBKAVICH, ISRAEL SANCHEZ, ERIC KIM, AMY KIM GANTER, LES McCLAINE, BEN HATKE, PAUL RIVOCHE, PHIL CRAVEN, NEIL BABRA, AND KAZU KIBUISHI.

Author portrait by Kazu Kibuishi

Printed in Singapore

First Disney • Hyperion edition, 2009
10 9 8 7 6 5 4 3 2 1

ISBN 978-1-4231-0565-7
Library of Congress Cataloging-in-Publication Data on file.

Visit www.hyperionbooksforchildren.com

CHAPTER SIX

THAT'S THE LAST OF THE SANDWICHES, SO DON'T EAT IT ALL AT ONCE, OKAY?

LOOK, I'M REALLY SORRY I PANICKED BACK ON THE TRAIN LIKE THAT, OKAY? I'M NOT SURE WHAT I WAS THINKING.

JELLABY, I WANT YOU TO TELL PORTIA THAT I'M NOT TALKING TO HER ANYMORE, NOT AFTER WHAT SHE PULLED.

AFTER WHAT *I* PULLED? I WASN'T THE ONE WHO PUT US IN THAT POSITION IN THE FIRST PLACE!

WELL, JELLABY, YOU CAN TELL JASON THAT HE'S BEING A JERK...

...AND IF HE'S NOT GOING TO LISTEN, THEN I'M NOT GOING TO TALK TO HIM EITHER!

PORTIA, WAIT!

JELLABY, LET'S GO!

13

COME ON, WE GOTTA GET OUT OF HERE RIGHT NOW!

HEY! WHAT GIVES?

HONNK HOONK

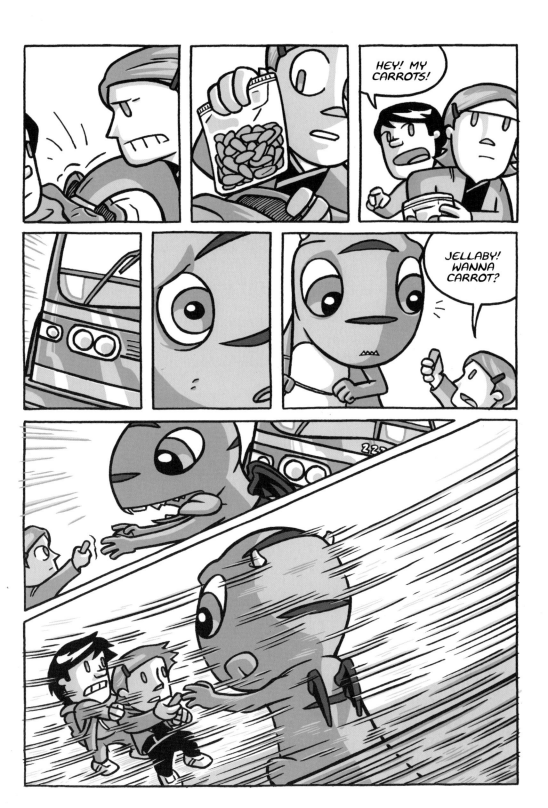

SO MUCH FOR
MY CARROTS.

SO...

...WHICH
WAY ARE WE
HEADED NOW?

THAT WAY.

UH, NO. IT'S THIS WAY, I THINK.

YOU *THINK*? YOU MEAN YOU'RE NOT SURE?

WELL, I *DID* BRING A MAP WITH ME, BUT IT WAS IN THE BAG WE LEFT ON THE TRAIN...

OH MAN.

YOU HAVE *GOT* TO BE KIDDING ME.

LOOK, THIS ISN'T THAT BAD. ALL WE NEED TO DO IS FIND A BOOKSTORE AND FIND A—

HEY!

WHAT ARE YOU KIDS DOING, SITTING IN THE MIDDLE OF THE SIDEWALK?

OH, SORRY. WE WERE JUST ABOUT TO GET GOING.

!

GOING TO THE HALLOWEEN FAIR, ARE WE?

YOU'VE DONE A GREAT JOB WITH THIS COSTUME.

OH, UM, THANKS. WE MADE IT OURSELVES.

POKE POKE

UH, WE HAVE TO GET GOING. WE'RE MEETING SOME FRIENDS AT THAT BOOKSTORE.

AGAIN, WE'RE TERRIBLY SORRY.

HE'S NOT FOLLOWING US.

THAT'S A RELIEF.

OVER HERE.

CREEEEAAK

CAN I TRUST YOU GUYS TO BEHAVE YOURSELVES FOR A FEW MINUTES WHILE I CHECK THE MAPS?

YEAH, YEAH.

OKAY.

...SO IN THE END, HORTON HATCHES THE EGG, SEE?

OKAY, I THINK I FIGURED IT OUT.

WE'RE HERE. EXHIBITION PLACE IS OVER THERE.

ALL WE NEED TO DO IS FOLLOW THE STREET WE'RE ON NOW ALL THE WAY DOWN TO STRACHAN, AND THAT'LL TAKE US RIGHT TO THE EX.

SOUNDS SIMPLE ENOUGH.

RIGHT. LET'S GET GOING, THEN.

PORTIA, YOU OKAY?

I'M FINE.

26

STAY CLOSE, OKAY?

CHAPTER SEVEN

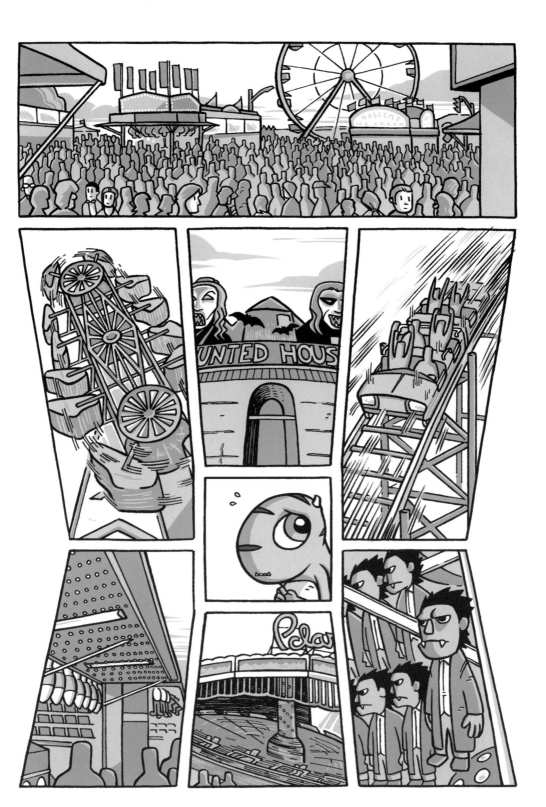

MAN, THIS PLACE IS *HUGE*. WHERE ARE WE SUPPOSED TO START LOOKING FOR THAT DOOR?

I DON'T KNOW.

I SUPPOSE WE HAVE TO START SOME- WHERE. WHY DON'T WE...

JELLABY!
WHAT ARE
YOU DOING?
COME ON
ALREADY.

WE SHOULD BE LOOKING FOR THAT DOOR OF YOURS.

WE FIGURE THE AUTOMOTIVE BUILDING MIGHT BE A GOOD PLACE TO START.

GBBBRRRR

AND, UH...

GBBRBRRRRR

YOU'RE HUNGRY? *AGAIN?* CAN'T IT WAIT FOR JUST A LITTLE LONGER?

YOU KNOW, THAT ISN'T SUCH A BAD IDEA! IT'S BEEN AGES SINCE LUNCH.

YOU GUYS ARE TERRIBLE.

GBBRRR

WELL, I SUPPOSE WE COULD GET SOMETHING TO EAT.

BUT WHERE ARE WE GOING TO FIND...?

OH.

FOOD

THAT'S A BIT OBVIOUS.

*—A BUILDING WITH THAT SIGN REALLY DOES EXIST. —K.

HANG ON.

WE SHOULD PROBABLY TRY TO KEEP YOU OUT OF SIGHT. THE LESS ATTENTION WE DRAW, THE BETTER.

BESIDES, WHO KNOWS WHAT YOU'LL DO IN A BUILDING FULL OF FOOD.

SIGH.

JASON, DO YOU THINK YOU COULD GET SOME FOOD FOR US?

YEAH, NO PROBLEM. I'LL BE BACK IN A JIFFY.

COME ON, LET'S WAIT FOR HIM OVER HERE.

JELLABY...

I'M SORRY ABOUT ALL THIS. IT HASN'T BEEN MUCH OF AN ADVENTURE SO FAR, HAS IT?

I JUST...

I JUST THOUGHT IT WAS GOING TO BE MORE FUN THAN THIS, YOU KNOW?

AND I, UH....

I GUESS I HAVEN'T DONE A GREAT JOB LOOKING OUT FOR YOU, HAVE I?

I DON'T EVEN KNOW HOW WE'RE GOING TO FIND THAT DOOR IN ALL OF THIS.

YOU KNOW...

I MISS MY DAD.

I DON'T KNOW WHY HE WOULD JUST DISAPPEAR LIKE HE DID...SOMETIMES I WISH I COULD TALK TO MOM ABOUT IT. THERE ARE DAYS WHEN SHE GETS THAT LOOK, YOU KNOW?

I WANT TO DO SOMETHING TO HELP, BUT I JUST DON'T KNOW WHAT I CAN DO. IT—IT JUST HURTS TO SEE HER LIKE THAT.

IF DAD WAS HERE, HE'D KNOW THE RIGHT THING TO SAY TO MAKE IT BETTER.

40

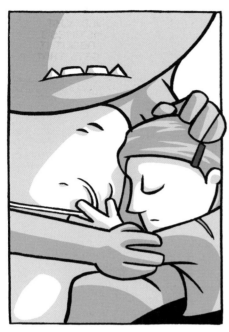

HERE, I WANT YOU TO HAVE THIS.

I WON'T LET ANYTHING HAPPEN TO YOU, I PROMISE.

AHEM—

FOOD, ANYONE?

HEY...

WHAT *IS* THIS?

OH, THAT? THEY'RE CORN DOGS. BASICALLY HOT DOGS FRIED IN BATTER.

UGH, THAT SOUNDS TERRIBLE.

JUST GIVE IT A TRY! IT'S GOOD.

I DUNNO...

OH WELL.

CHEW CHEW

GULP!

HEY!

THIS ISN'T BAD AT ALL!

SEE? I TOLD YOU.

HEY, CAN I ASK...?

YEAH?

HOW ARE YOU ABLE TO AFFORD ALL THIS? I MEAN, THE TICKETS, THE FOOD... THAT CAN'T BE CHEAP.

OH. WELL, I HAD SOME MONEY SAVED UP FOR THAT NEW MARIO GAME I WANTED, BUT I FIGURED IT'S NOT AS BIG A DEAL AS THIS IS.

OH.

REALLY? WHY WOULD YOU DO THAT FOR US?

I DUNNO. YOU MEAN I CAN'T BE NICE FOR NO REASON?

AFTER ALL, THAT DOOR ISN'T GOING TO FIND ITSELF.

OOOH, PORTIA! LET'S GO ON THIS RIDE!

HEY, FOCUS, FOCUS! WE DON'T HAVE TIME FOR RIDES!

YEAH, BUT WHEN ARE WE GONNA BE BACK HERE AGAIN? DON'T BE SUCH A STICK-IN-THE-MUD.

C'MOOOON, JUST ONE RIDE!

FINE. YOU GUYS GO THEN, IF YOU WANT TO SO BAD.

NO, YOU GUYS GO ON. I'LL WAIT FOR YOU HERE.

TUG TUG

WHAT'RE YOU, SCARED?

OF COURSE I'M NOT SCARED. IT'S JUST THAT THIS RIDE IS SILLY, THAT'S ALL.

FINE. COME ON, JELLABY.

ALL RIGHT, ALL RIGHT. I'LL GO.

THIS IS A BIG MISTAKE, THOUGH...

CREEEEEEEEAK...

CLACK.

CLANK
CLANK
CLANK

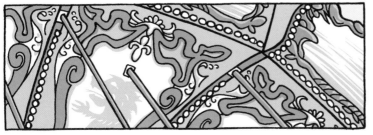

HEY, CHECK OUT THE MIDWAY! ISN'T IT AWESOME?

UH-HUH.

WHOA.

CHAPTER EIGHT

OH MAN, THAT WAS PRETTY AWESOME.

YEAH? SO WHICH RIDE SHOULD WE GO ON NEXT?

WELL, I WAS THINKING WE COULD TRY—

WE'RE GOING IN HERE.

WHAT? WHY?

EXCUSE US.

THE GUY NEEDS TO GET A NEW ACT.

EXCUSE ME...

NO, NO, I'VE TOLD YOU BEFORE, I DON'T DO BIRTHDAYS. NOW RUN ALONG, OR I—

UM, HI. I'M JASON, AND THAT'S PORTIA OVER THERE. AND THIS GUY HERE IS JELLABY.

...COULD IT BE?

AFTER ALL THIS TIME?

HOW DID YOU FIND HIM?

WELL, WE—

NO, WAIT.

YOU FOUND HIM...IN THE WOODS? YOU HAVE TRAVELED FAR TO COME HERE. YOU BROUGHT HIM HERE TO HELP HIM FIND HIS WAY HOME.

GEEZ, HOW DID YOU DO THAT?

HOW DID HE DO THAT?

CAN YOU GUESS THE NUMBER I'M THINKING OF?

OH, FOR—KNOCK IT OFF, HE'S NOT A MIND READER!

ACTUALLY...

SORRY, BUT I REALLY NEED TO TALK TO MY FRIEND RIGHT NOW. EXCUSE US.

THERE'S SOMETHING ABOUT HIM THAT I DON'T TRUST.

WHAT'S NOT TO TRUST? HE SEEMS LIKE A NICE ENOUGH GUY.

JUST A FEELING I HAVE.

WHAT IS WRONG WITH YOU? WHY CAN'T YOU JUST TRUST SOMEONE ELSE FOR A CHANGE?

YOU WANT ME TO TRUST HIM? JUST BECAUSE HE CAN DO A FEW TRICKS AND MAKE SOME EDUCATED GUESSES?

DON'T BE SO STUPID. THERE'S NO SUCH THING AS MAGIC!

GEEZ. NO WONDER YOU DON'T HAVE ANY FRIENDS.

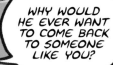

YEAH, YOU'RE RIGHT! THERE'S NO SUCH THING AS MAGIC! YOU WISH ALL YOU WANT, IT'LL NEVER BRING YOUR DAD BACK!

WHY WOULD HE EVER WANT TO COME BACK TO SOMEONE LIKE YOU?

NO.
DON'T.

SNRK.

HEY, ARE YOU OKAY?

REMEMBER US? WE STILL OWE YOU FROM THE OTHER DAY.

WELL, WELL. LOOK WHO IT IS.

I DON'T HAVE TIME FOR THIS. OR FOR YOU.

HEY. YOU'RE NOT GOING ANY-WHERE.

YEAH? OR WHAT? YOU GOING TO HIT ME? *A GIRL?* IN FRONT OF ALL THESE PEOPLE?

WELL, YOU'D BETTER HURRY IT UP AND GET IT DONE, BECAUSE I'VE GOT MORE IMPORTANT THINGS TO DO.

CHAPTER NINE

WOW.

WE ARE ALMOST THERE.

SHE WILL BE JOINING US SHORTLY.

"SHE?" "SHE" WHO?

YOU WILL FIND OUT SOON ENOUGH.

TRY NOT TO DISAPPOINT HER.

HELLO?

IS ANYONE OUT THERE?

CLUNK

JELLABY, IS THAT YOU?

CLANK

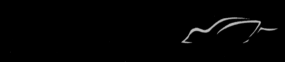

OH.

WHAT ARE YOU LOOKING FOR BACK THERE?

HERE YOU GO.

THANK YOU, CHILD.

MIGHT I VENTURE A QUESTION?

WHAT ARE YOU DOING IN THIS PLACE? TURN BACK AT ONCE. IT IS NOT SAFE HERE.

UM, HI?

HELLO! DO...YOU... UNDERSTAND...ME?

OR PERHAPS YOU ARE ONE OF THOSE SLOW CHILDREN? HEAVENS ME, IN THIS DAY AND AGE.

WHAT? NO, I'M NOT SLOW.

UH, I MEAN... I'M LOOKING FOR MY FRIENDS. HAVE YOU SEEN THEM? ONE IS A LOUD, OBNOXIOUS BOY, AND THE OTHER IS A BIG, UM, PURPLE ...THING.

HRM. YES. YES, THEY PASSED THROUGH HERE NOT LONG AGO. THEY ARE BEING TAKEN TO HER.

"HER?"

"HER" WHO?

HELLO?

HELLO. IT IS A PLEASURE TO MEET YOU. I AM XOLOTL.

I, UM. YEAH. HI. I-I'M JASON. AND THIS IS JELLABY.

HELLO, JASON.

JELLABY.

WELL, YOU CERTAINLY MUST HAVE TRAVELED A LONG WAY TO GET HERE, I'M SURE.

PLEASE, REST.

SO, UH, YOU KNOW HOW TO GET JELLABY HOME?

ALL IN GOOD TIME, ALL IN GOOD TIME.

TELL ME, DO YOU LIKE TO READ?

NOT REALLY. I DO LIKE VIDEO GAMES, THOUGH.

AH, I WAS JUST HOPING YOU COULD PROVIDE MORE... STIMULATING CONVERSATION.

IS THAT ALL YOU'LL BE NEEDING OF ME?

YES, YES. THAT WILL BE ALL FOR NOW.

SO, UH, HOW DID YOU END UP DOWN HERE? IT'S...KIND OF RUN DOWN.

WELL...

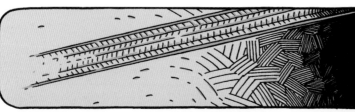

AND EVER SINCE THEN SHE HAS BEEN SEARCHING FOR ANOTHER TO TAKE HIS PLACE.

SHE HAS NOT BEEN SUCCESSFUL.

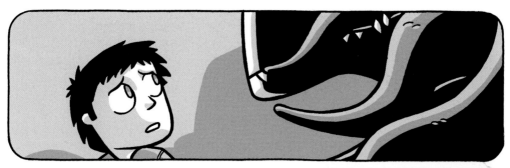

XOLOTL IS MUCH OLDER NOW. DECADES AGO, SHE FOUND THIS PLACE HIDDEN UNDER THE GROUND AND HID HERSELF FROM THE WORLD. BUT HER ANGER STILL REMAINS.

AND IT IS HER TEMPER THAT MAKES HER TRULY DANGEROUS.

93

YOU DON'T HAVE TO WORRY ABOUT ANYTHING ANYMORE. EVERYTHING WILL TAKE CARE OF ITSELF IN TIME.

YOUR FRIEND JASON.

SHE WILL TRY TO MAKE HIM HERS.

AND IF SHE CANNOT HAVE THAT, SHE WILL DESTROY HIM.

IT MAY
ALREADY
BE TOO
LATE.

CHAPTER TEN

DAD?

PORTIA.

SHHH. THERE'LL BE PLENTY OF TIME FOR THAT. I'LL EXPLAIN EVERYTHING SOON ENOUGH.

COME.

WAIT. I THINK THERE'S SOMETHING I HAVE TO DO FIRST.

OH, IT'S PROBABLY NOTHING.

CAREFUL NOW, DON'T GIVE THEM TOO MUCH.

OKAY.

REMEMBER THAT TIME IN THE SQUARE WHEN ALL THE BIRDS LANDED ON YOU AND WENT AFTER THE BIRDSEED YOU HAD?

AWW, DAAAD. DON'T REMIND ME.

HA HA, OKAY, OKAY.

SO, DAD...

HMM?

YOU, UH...

YOU HAVEN'T ASKED ABOUT MOM YET.

SO...HOW IS YOUR MOM?

OH, SHE'S OKAY.

NO, I DON'T THINK SHE IS.

SHE DOESN'T TALK ABOUT IT, BUT I KNOW SHE MISSES YOU.

I DO TOO.

ARE...

...ARE YOU AND MOM FIGHTING?

PORTIA...

...WHY RUIN A PERFECT DAY WORRYING ABOUT SOMETHING LIKE THAT?

...

YOU'RE RIGHT, I GUESS.

YOU'RE RIGHT.

THAT'S MY GIRL.

THAT'S MY GIRL...

...AND THESE CARVINGS I MADE MYSELF.

HUH, THAT'S... NICE.

AND THERE IS PLENTY TO EXPLORE AROUND HERE.

THE TUNNELS DOWN HERE ARE SO MAZELIKE THAT YOU COULD LOSE YOURSELF IN THEM FOR MONTHS, AND STILL NEVER SEE IT ALL.

THAT DOES SOUND KIND OF COOL.

SO, UH... WHEN ARE WE GOING TO BE TAKING JELLABY HOME?

HOME? HA HA HA! OH MY DEAR BOY, THAT IS PRECIOUS.

WAIT, WHAT?

DON'T YOU THINK IF I HAD THE SLIGHTEST IDEA AS TO WHERE "HOME" WAS, THAT I WOULD'VE LEFT THIS PLACE BY NOW?

W-WHAT ARE YOU SAYING?

DO YOU ACTUALLY THINK IT WAS A COINCIDENCE THAT YOU ENDED UP HERE, ONLY TO FIND ME?

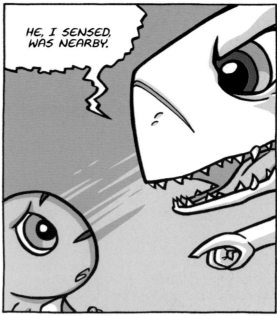

HE, I SENSED, WAS NEARBY.

AND WITH THOSE LIKE HIM, THERE ARE ALWAYS CHILDREN.

YOU...YOU PLANNED THIS?

WHY, OF COURSE, MY DEAR BOY. I HAVE WAYS OF BRINGING YOU HERE.

109

HISSSS

FLAP
FLAP

OH,
HELLO.

YOU DON'T UNDERSTAND. I CAN'T JUST LEAVE HIM LIKE THAT.

I GAVE HIM MY WORD.

COME ON PORTIA, EVERYONE BREAKS A PROMISE NOW AND AGAIN. THEY'RE JUST WORDS, AFTER ALL.

NO. NO, YOU'RE WRONG.

BECAUSE I'M NOT LIKE THAT. MY FRIENDS NEED ME RIGHT NOW.

NO. STAY.

NO! LET
GO OF ME!

STAAAAY

PORTIAAA...

COME
BAAACK...

SNAP

SLIP!

HSSSAAAAA

AGHH!

TRIP!

WHUMP!

HISSSSSS

JELLABY.

Y-YOU'RE CRAZY.

WHAT?

YOU CAN'T JUST *TELL* PEOPLE THEY'RE YOUR FRIENDS. IT DOESN'T WORK LIKE THAT.

UHM, LOOK, WE'RE REALLY SORRY ABOUT WASTING YOUR TIME, BUT I THINK MAYBE JELLABY AND I SHOULD GET GOING...

WAIT—

GRROWWWL

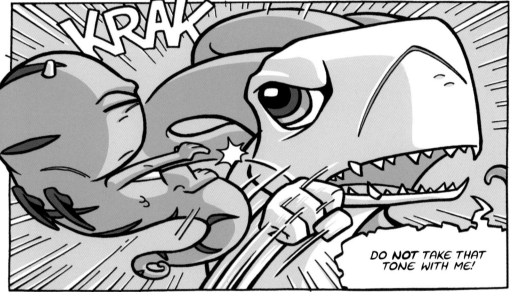

NOW, WHERE WERE WE?

YOU— YOU...!

OH, DON'T BE SO MELODRAMATIC. WE ARE A TOUGH BREED.

YOU, ON THE OTHER HAND...

NO!

YOU ARE BEGINNING TO TRY MY PATIENCE.

CRUNCH

STOP!

I'LL DO WHAT YOU WANT! JUST STOP HURTING HIM!

GOOD. NOW WHY DON'T WE—EH?

SNAP!

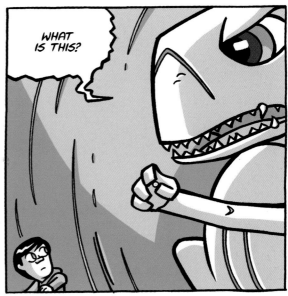

WHAT IS THIS?

I-IT'S A RING.

I KNOW IT'S A RING. WHAT IS ITS IMPORTANCE?

HOW SHOULD I KNOW?

YOU'RE LYING.

IT'S A SECRET DECODER RING.

KRAK

HA HA HA

I FOUND IT AT THE BOTTOM OF A CEREAL BOX.

CHAPTER ELEVEN

LET THEM GO.

HA! WHAT A DELIGHTFUL LITTLE FIREBRAND YOU ARE, MY DEAR.

YOU ARE HARDLY IN A POSITION TO MAKE DEMANDS.

WELL, YOU'RE NOT GOING TO MAKE MANY FRIENDS IF YOU CRUSH THEM ALL.

OOOF.

WELL, YOU'VE CERTAINLY CONVINCED ME.

GOOD. NOW LET THEM GO.

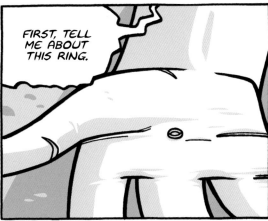

FIRST, TELL ME ABOUT THIS RING.

AND MAYBE THEN I'LL CONSIDER IT.

IT'S...

IT'S WHAT I USED TO MAKE JELLABY MINE.

THE RING—IT'S A SYMBOL OF MY OWNERSHIP OVER HIM.

EVEN WHEN I TRIED TO LEAVE HIM WITH JASON, I COULDN'T STAY APART FROM JELLABY. I-IT'S WHY I HAD TO COME BACK FOR HIM, YOU SEE.

BUT THE OWNER OF THE RING—ME—HAS TO GIVE IT AWAY VOLUNTARILY FOR IT TO WORK.

I-I COULD GIVE IT TO YOU INSTEAD, IF YOU LIKE.

NOW WHY WOULD YOU DO SOMETHING LIKE THAT?

I'LL DO IT IF IT MEANS YOU'LL STOP HURTING THEM.

BESIDES, YOU'RE OBVIOUSLY FAR MORE INTELLIGENT THAN JELLABY IS.

I MEAN, YOU KNOW HOW TO *SPEAK*, FOR ONE.

AND IT *DOES* SEEM INTERESTING DOWN HERE.

I COULD GET TO LIKE IT HERE, I THINK.

ISN'T THAT WHAT YOU WANT?

VERY WELL.

JASON! JELLABY! ARE YOU GUYS OKAY?

PORTIA, YOUR DAD'S RING—

I KNOW. COME ON, WE'VE GOT TO GET OUT OF HERE.

AND HURRY!

BOM BOM BOM BOM

MAN, YOU THINK SHE'LL BE OKAY?

HEY! DIDN'T YOU HEAR PORTIA? WE SHOULD GO GET HELP!

HEY! WAIT UP!

OH NO.

PORTIA!

WHAT ARE YOU DOING UP THERE?

WE CAME TO HELP!

...I THINK WE TOOK A WRONG TURN SOMEWHERE.

NEVER MIND THAT NOW, JUST HURRY!

I-I CAN'T REACH!

IT'S XOLOTL! HIDE!

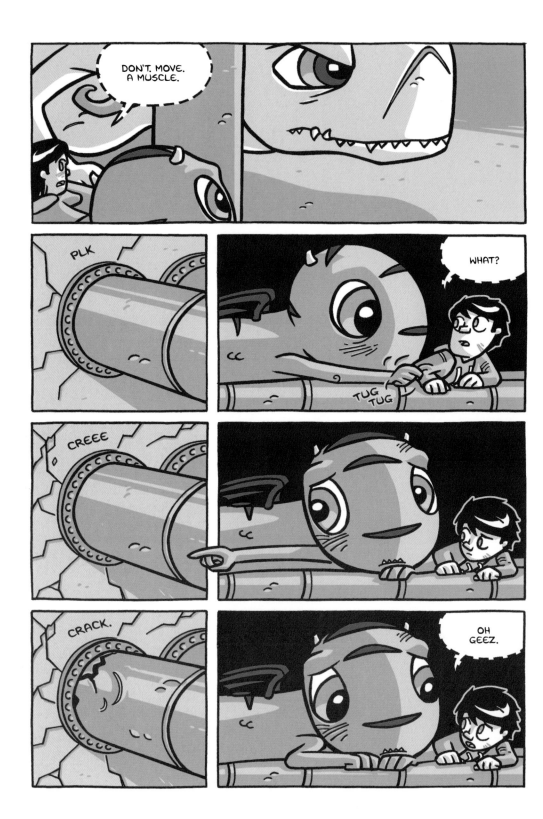

SQUEEE

BE LIGHTER!
BE LIGHTER!

CHUNG.

FLAP
FLAP

FLAP
FLAP

IT'S
WORKING!

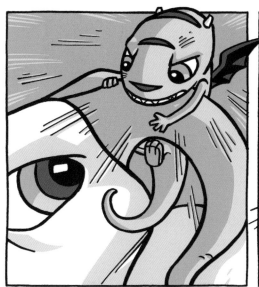

RAAAAAAAA

GRROOAR

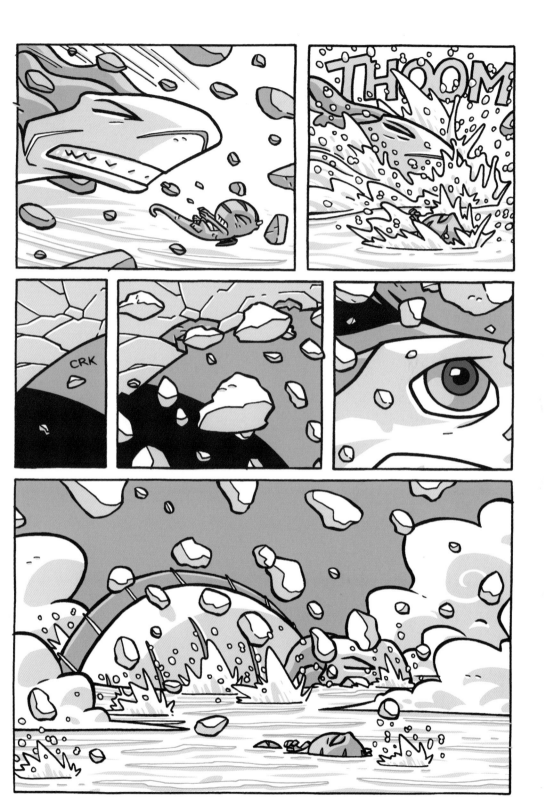

JELLABY!

YOU OKAY?

NOD!

UH, GUYS...I THINK WE'D BETTER GET OUT OF HERE.

PORTIA, COME ON.

HURRY!

PORTIA... I...

JASON!

COME ON! GET UP, *GET UP!*

FLOP!

GEEZ...

SOMEBODY'S GOING TO BE REALLY MAD.

JASON? JELLABY? I-I WANT YOU TO KNOW I'M SORRY FOR LEAVING YOU GUYS.

I WAS BEING SELFISH. I'M REALLY SORRY.

AW, DON'T SWEAT IT. THANKS FOR COMING BACK FOR US.

AND I...UH, I'M SORRY ABOUT THE THINGS I SAID ABOUT YOUR DAD.

IT'S OKAY. REALLY.

FRIENDS?

FRIENDS.

...

PEOPLE ARE GOING TO BE HERE ANY MINUTE.

YOU'D BETTER GET OUT OF SIGHT, AND QUICK.

WE'LL FIND YOU ONCE WE GET THIS ALL SORTED OUT.

NOD!

EPILOGUE

HERALD

Building Collapse

Crews conti
search, one
occupant st
missing

I'M SO GLAD YOU'RE HOME SAFE. YOU WOULDN'T BELIEVE HOW WORRIED I WAS!

I WAS ANGRY TOO, YOU KNOW? I WOULD'VE TAKEN YOU TO THE FAIR IF YOU REALLY WANTED TO GO.

I KNOW. I'M SORRY.

MOM? REMEMBER WHEN YOU SAID YOU DIDN'T WANT ME TO KEEP ANY SECRETS FROM YOU?

YES?

WELL...I FOUND THAT BOX THAT YOU HAVE OF DAD'S THINGS.

I-I TOOK A RING OF HIS...

AND I KIND OF...LOST IT.

I'M REALLY SORRY. YOU... YOU'RE NOT MAD, ARE YOU?

I JUST...I JUST REALLY MISS DAD.

OH, BABY.

I MISS HIM, TOO.

-SNF- THERE'S SOMETHING ELSE I HAVE TO TELL YOU.

YES?

IT'S, UH...IT'S PROBABLY EASIER IF I JUST SHOW YOU.

WAIT RIGHT THERE, OKAY?

SLIDE

HEY, ARE YOU READY? IT'S TIME TO MEET MY—

AAAHH!

WHAT ARE YOU DOING? DON'T EAT THAT! TAKE THAT OUT OF YOUR MOUTH RIGHT NOW!